The Angry Birds Movie 2: 2020
A CENTUM BOOK 978-1-913072-33-9
Published in Great Britain by Centum Books Ltd
This edition published 2019
1 3 5 7 9 10 8 6 4 2

Centum Books Ltd, 20 Devon Square, Newton Abbot, Devon, TQ12 2HR, UK

books@centumbooksltd.co.uk

CENTUM BOOKS Limited Reg. No. 07641486

A CIP catalogue record for this book is available from the British Library.

Printed in Poland.

centum

RED: LEADER OF THE FLOCK

Cranky, sarcastic and downright angry, this hot-headed bird with enormous eyebrows is an unlikely hero. A very unlikely hero. But hero he is – ever since he battled the pigs and rescued the birds' precious eggs.

Not very long ago, Red was an outsider who thought he was different from the others. Everyone agreed – and not in a good way.

Things changed after he faced those scheming pigs. But even though he's red-hot with pride after saving Bird Village, he can't quite shake off the feeling that he's still the odd bird out.

LIKES
- Being left alone
- Peace and quiet
- Protecting the eggs
- Being right

DISLIKES
- Pigs
- Danger to the flock
- Loud, friendly types
- Fakes and frauds
- Phoney friends

CHUCK: THE SPEED DEMON

LIKES
- Making friends
- Attention
- Doing everything at a million miles a minute
- Being impulsive
- Sports

DISLIKES
- Slowing down
- Slow eaters
- Speeding tickets
- Looking before he leaps

Special Skill: Super speed

He's a hyperactive, competitive show-off. What's not to love?

As the speediest bird on Bird Island, Chuck thinks fast, talks fast and moves like lightning. His best friends are Red and Bomb, and he's also Mighty Eagle's biggest fan. (We're talking super crazy fandom here!) He's as quick at making friends as he is on his feet, and he's super loyal.

Chuck's foolhardy choices and rash remarks often get him into hot water. Luckily, he's quick enough to get out of (almost) any trouble.

BOMB: SHORT FUSE

Special Skill: Exploding

This dim bulb has a big heart. The trouble is, he tends to blow up when he has big feelings.

Bomb has IED (Intermittent Explosive Disorder), which makes him detonate when he's angry or excited ... or scared, surprised or stressed. He'd love to be able to control himself – and he's working on it.

This charming bird has a wicked sense of humour, and he's a loyal friend. He takes things slowly and carefully, because he knows what happens if he gets too excited.

LIKES
- Having fun
- Blowing stuff up
- Being with friends

DISLIKES
- Being left out
- Being called a 'freak' of nature

MIGHTY EAGLE: LIVING LEGEND

LIKES
• Himself
• Being admired
• The sound of his own voice
• His glory days
• Saving the day

DISLIKES
• Being questioned
• Taking responsibility
• Leaving his cave
• Being called a 'has-been'

Special Skill: Flying, strength

A big bird with an even bigger ego, this one-time hero doesn't seem to have noticed that his days of glory are in the past.

Mighty Eagle is the only bird who has ever managed to fly. Every hatchling on the island knows the songs and stories of his epic adventures. When he's not boasting about the good old days, he spends his time on Eagle Mountain in the Hall of Heroism, a museum he built to celebrate his own achievements.

But behind his larger-than-life personality, Mighty Eagle has lost his confidence. He would rather hide in the past than live in the present.

SILVER: THE BRAINIAC

Special Skill: Quick thinking

This whip-smart student is always top of the class!

Chuck's little sister, Silver, is studying for an engineering degree at the Avian Academy. She's fizzing with energy and enthusiasm, and her inventive mind can solve complicated puzzles in the blink of an eye.

Silver is wise and clever, but she's not too grown up to join in a good old-fashioned tickle fight with her big brother.

LIKES
- Maths and science
- Piggy technology
- Being playful

DISLIKES
- Liars
- Grumpiness
- Being called a kid

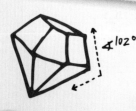

HATCHLINGS:
CUTENESS OVERLOAD

Special Skill: Making mischief

Curious, clueless and chaotic, these baby Angry Birds long to be part of every adventure.

Zoe, Vivi and Sam-Sam want to be just like their hero, Red, but somehow they always end up in a fluffy ball of trouble.

LIKES
- Exploring
- Having fun

DISLIKES
- Being left out
- Getting lost

HARVEY:
THE TROJAN EAGLE

Special Skill: hiding or disguising the team

Everyone's hoping that this feathery fake will help them to sneak past the giant eagles without being seen.

Inside Harvey, different parts of the costume are controlled by different members of the team.

What could possibly go wrong?

11

LEONARD: THE LYIN' KING

Special Skill: Smooth-talking

King Leonard is the charming, charismatic leader of the pigs. Though he speaks with sincerity and enthusiasm, the inhabitants of Bird Island have learned not to trust him – or his little green cohorts!

But when this larger-than-life character arrives on Red's doorstep with a story about a super-weapon designed to destroy life on both their islands, Red has no choice but to believe him.

LIKES
- Lunch
- Being in charge
- Scheming

DISLIKES
- Birds
- Disobedience

GARRY: THE PIG INVENTOR

Special Skill: Gadget maker

This arrogant inventor has created many tools to help his piggy teammates. There's just one problem: they're not very good. His favourite inventions are the flame-retardant pig-snot and the eagle-proximity detector.

COURTNEY: LEONARD'S ASSISTANT

Special Skill: Putting up with Leonard

Courtney spends more time texting on her phone and listening to music than actually working, but she's still the best assistant Leonard has ever had – which isn't saying much.

ZETA: THE CHILLIN' VILLAIN

Special Skill: Selfishness

The bitter ice queen of Eagle Island is fed up with the cold life.

Zeta is the leader of the eagles, and she has had enough of shivering on a frozen rock. She is obsessed with warm weather, and dreams of sipping cool drinks on the tropical beaches of Bird Island and Piggy Island.

This sarcastic, vain eagle stands out in a crowd, but she's always scowling. She loves sunsets, long walks and being mean. Most of all, she loves the idea that one day she might be able to leave Eagle Island for somewhere with hot showers.

LIKES
- Warm, tropical weather
- Piña coladas
- Swimming

DISLIKES
- Shivering
- Disloyalty
- Living on a frozen rock

DEBBIE:
PAID BEST FRIEND

Special Skill: Flattery

Zeta's clumsy assistant adores her purple-maned boss, and she's always ready with a hot meal and a cold drink. Whether she's fetching Zeta's ice slippers or acting as her chair, she's a loyal and trustworthy companion.

GLENN:
EAGLE SCIENTIST

Special Skill: Engineering

It's Glenn's job to bring Zeta's idea of a super weapon to life. Other scientists have tried and failed before him, and he doesn't want to suffer their fate. Glenn's hoping that he will be the one to make Zeta's dreams come true.

PIGGY ISLAND

Welcome to the land of green! The home of the pigs lies beyond the horizon. (Just watch out for the shipwrecks in the lagoon.) These clueless creatures have one thing in common – they would do anything for their greedy king. Cheerful and ready to obey orders, the pigs love nothing more than building – the more complicated the better!

PIG CITY

The pigs built their city in the central valley of the island, and they've been adding to it ever since. This has given the city an impressive look of barely organised chaos. A huge boulder on top of a house is a sign of high social status.

THE CASTLE

The royal castle is a jumbled mish-mash of rooms and towers. No one would dare to call the king a show-off, but the castle's golden decorations include a crown on top of the central tower, which holds up the biggest boulder in the city.

PIG LAB

Garry's state-of-the-art Pig Lab is hidden inside an enormous yellow submarine. Piggy scientists are always hard at work, and the lab produces an endless stream of super-cool gadgets.

EAGLE ISLAND

This freezing island spends all year under a thick layer of ice and snow. Because the eagles who live there can fly, all the buildings are super-tall. The eagles build their nests in the fir trees, but Zeta has made her chilly lair inside the volcano at the heart of the island.

ZETA'S LAIR

Eagle Island's active volcano is the perfect home for Zeta. From here, she has a great view of Bird and Piggy Islands, so her jealousy gets stronger every day. Her home looks exactly like a tropical island paradise, complete with palm trees, but it's all fake. Nearly everything here is built from ice.

THE SUPER WEAPON

The volcano's fiery lava powers Zeta's super weapon. It's a work of art made of swirling ramps and giant balls of ice.

BIRD ISLAND

This amazing island has something for every bird, from the wild jungle to the busy village. The birds who live here are a happy community, and they're not going to let pesky pigs or envious eagles spoil that. These feathery heroes never forget what really matters: family, friendship and being true to themselves.

BIRD VILLAGE

The village lies at the heart of Bird Island. Whether they're shopping, working or meeting friends, the birds of the island can be found here every day. Main Street gets very busy, but officers are always there to keep the community safe.

AVIAN ACADEMY

The island's brightest birds flock to the Avian Academy to learn and be inspired. It's bursting with classrooms, study halls and outdoor spaces, which makes it the perfect place for brainy birds like Silver to expand their knowledge.

How many hatchlings are scampering around these pages?

Visitor's Questionnaire

What do you like best about Bird Island? _____

Favourite fast food – worms or bugs? _____

If you ran the island, how would you keep the pigs away? _____

_____

Who's your favourite Angry Bird? _____

Answers on page 50

CHUCK'S FAST FACTS

Chuck has ten quick-fire 'facts' for you –
can you keep up and tell fact from fiction?

1. Red loves hugs.   True ◯ False ⊘

2. Eggs are Leonard's favourite food.   True ⊘ False ◯

3. Bomb's feet get cold when he's angry.   True ◯ False ⊘

4. Zeta lives in a volcano.   True ◯ False ⊘

5. Garry is an inventor.   True ◯ False ⊘

6. Courtney is Zeta's assistant.   True ⊘ False ◯

7. The speediest thing about Silver is her brain. True ⊘ False ◯

8. Glenn is working on a super weapon.   True ⊘ False ◯

9. Debbie goes to the Avian Academy.   True ◯ False ⊘

10. Mighty Eagle lives on Eagle Island.   True ◯ False ⊘

Answers on page 50

KNOW YOURSELF!

Are you a bird or a pig? Answer these questions to find out who you are most like.

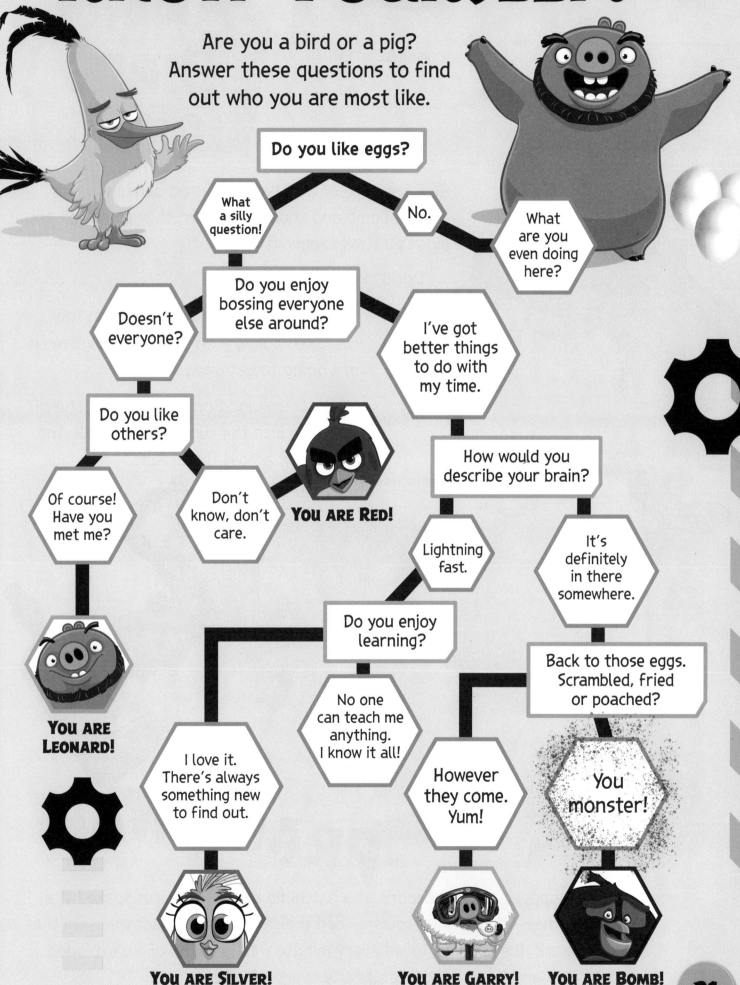

Do you like eggs?

What a silly question!

No.

What are you even doing here?

Do you enjoy bossing everyone else around?

Doesn't everyone?

I've got better things to do with my time.

Do you like others?

Don't know, don't care.

YOU ARE RED!

How would you describe your brain?

Of course! Have you met me?

Lightning fast.

It's definitely in there somewhere.

YOU ARE LEONARD!

Do you enjoy learning?

No one can teach me anything. I know it all!

Back to those eggs. Scrambled, fried or poached?

I love it. There's always something new to find out.

However they come. Yum!

You monster!

YOU ARE SILVER!

YOU ARE GARRY!

YOU ARE BOMB!

ANGRY BIRDS
Part One

Red, the hero of Bird Island, was on patrol with his friends Bomb and Chuck. Together, they could foil any piggy plot! Well, almost ...

"Duck!" Red yelled.

SPLAT! A cream pie hit a duck in the face. Red boiled with anger. The pigs were not going to get away with this!

Red, Chuck and Bomb loaded a bottle of hot sauce into the slingshot. **TWANG!** The bottle flew across the ocean ... and made a spicy splat.

PRANK WAR!

The pigs popped all the balloons at a hatchling party. The birds soaked the pigs with a massive belly-flop splash. Then the pigs dropped giant crabs on the birds. Leonard, the pig king, loved every minute – till a chunk of ice exploded onto Piggy Island Beach, and froze nearly everything solid.

"Where did that come from?" he squealed.

He peered through his telescope and saw a mysterious, icy island.

A SHORT TIME LATER, BACK ON BIRD ISLAND ...

A small, red balloon arrived with a letter tied to the string. It was from Leonard.

Dear Birds, we want a truce. Can we talk?

"It's another prank," scoffed Red.

But to his horror, the other birds believed Leonard.

"The Prank War is over," Bomb declared.

"The world doesn't need saving any more," said Chuck.

"It's a trick!" Red squawked.

But not a single bird would listen.

Zeta, the queen of Eagle Island, was lying on a frozen pool in her volcano lair and scheming. She wanted to use her ice-ball super weapon to scare the birds and pigs away from Bird Island and Piggy Island.

Everything about her kingdom was freezing, and Zeta was sick of it. Luckily, she knew exactly what would make her happy: palm trees, tropical breezes and sandy beaches.

At home, Red was feeling miserable. What if the island didn't need a hero any more? Would he go back to being a loser?

KNOCK KNOCK!

Red slid across the floor and opened the door. It was Leonard!

Red saw red. He tied Leonard up and stood on top of him.

"This is not how a truce works," said Leonard in a muffled voice. "Red, we've discovered that there's a third island and they are plotting to destroy us all!"

Leonard showed Red the photos that his special-ops pigs, Squeal Team 6, had snapped of Zeta in her lair. For the first time, Red and Leonard agreed on something. They had to stop fighting and work together to save the world!

To be continued ...

MIRROR, MIRROR

There's something wrong with this picture of Sam-Sam. It's only half finished! Can you complete the drawing and colour it in?

Don't panic, Bomb!

WORDSEARCH

Red has sent Bomb a coded message. The places that are most important to their mission are hidden in this grid. Can you help Bomb to find them all? Words can go forwards, backwards, up, down and diagonally, so you need to stay alert.

Z	J	A	I	L	C	I	E	Q	H
A	W	H	R	A	Q	M	L	P	N
V	C	U	A	I	K	F	T	O	I
O	L	A	B	R	F	G	S	V	A
L	Q	S	D	J	B	I	A	J	T
C	H	C	A	E	B	O	C	X	N
A	F	I	K	Y	M	Z	U	S	U
N	M	T	L	I	H	Y	J	R	O
O	X	Y	J	U	N	G	L	E	M
V	I	L	L	A	G	E	D	F	K

- [ ] LAB
- [ ] VOLCANO
- [ ] VILLAGE
- [ ] BEACH
- [ ] MOUNTAIN
- [ ] CITY
- [ ] HARBOUR
- [ ] JUNGLE
- [ ] JAIL
- [ ] CASTLE
- [ ] LAIR
- [ ] ACADEMY

27

Answers on page 50

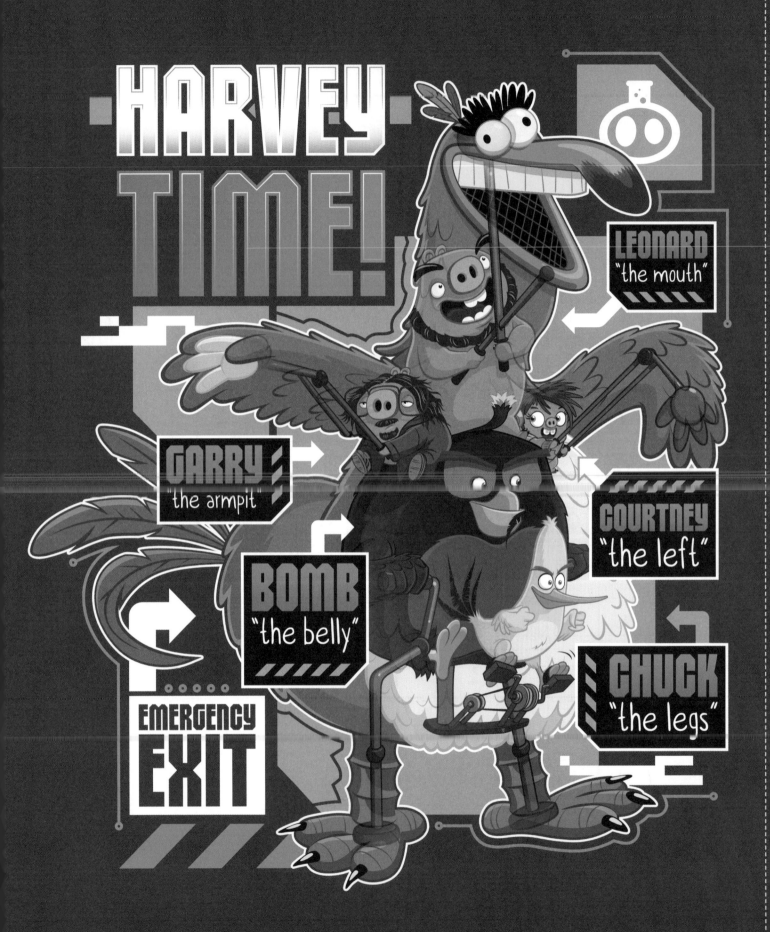

SPOT THE DIFFERENCE

Can you find all eight differences between these snaps of the Avian Academy?

Answers on page 51

MOBILE CHALLENGE

It's your mission to follow the instructions and make your own Angry Birds decoration.

EQUIPMENT

- Paper plate
- Sheets of white card
- Coloured ribbon
- Scissors
- Glue

Always ask an adult to help you when using scissors.

INSTRUCTIONS

1

Cut the paper plate in half.

2

Draw a picture of Bird Island on one side of each half.

3

Draw or trace pictures of your favourite characters onto the card. Make them as big or small as you wish.

4

Cut out the characters and glue each one to a piece of ribbon.

5

Glue the other end of the ribbon to the plain side of Bird Island.

6

Glue a ribbon loop to the top of your mobile.

7

Stick the two halves of Bird Island together joining the plain sides.

8

Hang your mobile close to a window, so it moves in the breeze.

PIGGY PUZZLE

How many special ops pigs are on Squeal Team 6?

Answers on page 51

There are ___ pigs.

SCHEMING SNORTER

Garry has written a list of everyone he wants to prank. Can you work out the names and warn the victims?

1. DR E
2. MOBB
3. LIVERS
4. CC HUK
5. TONY CURE
6. TAZE
7. BEE BID
8. I AM THE LEGGY
9. N LENG
10. CASH H GLINT

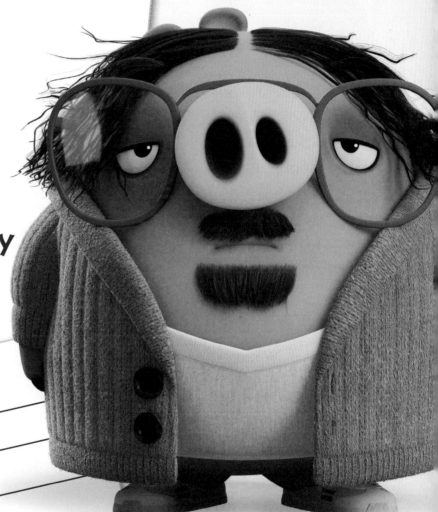

1. _____
2. _____
3. _____
4. _____
5. _____
6. _____
7. _____
8. _____
9. _____
10. _____

GENUINE
100% PURE
SWINE SLIME

ANGRY BIRDS
Part Two

Soon, the heist crew was ready. Red, Bomb, Chuck, Leonard and Mighty Eagle were all on the team, as well as Leonard's top scientist Garry, and Chuck's kid sister Silver. She was an engineering wizard brainiac, and had even invented something called Super String – the strongest string in the world. They met in Mighty Eagle's cave. Leonard and his assistant, Courtney, showed them maps and photos of Eagle Island and the volcano headquarters.

"This is their leader," Leonard said.

When Mighty Eagle saw Zeta, he gasped. Just then, there was a strange whistling sound from outside. A giant ice ball was hurtling towards them! Mighty Eagle zoomed out of his cave with the birds and pigs on his back.

CRASH!

The ice ball hit the top of Eagle Mountain and sent it crashing into the sea.

Over on Eagle Island, Zeta cackled with laughter to see Mighty Eagle's home destroyed. Her assistant, Debbie, cheered. Everything was going according to plan.

"Fill those ice balls with molten lava," Zeta barked at Glenn, the lead engineer.

She had to make the birds leave the island –

FOR EVER!

When the heist crew arrived on Eagle Island in Leonard's submarine, they were excited. The mission had begun! But suddenly, Mighty Eagle stopped.

"I know Zeta," he admitted.

He explained that he had left her on their wedding day, which was why she was such an angry bird.

"It's all my fault," said Mighty Eagle miserably. "She's been heartbroken ever since."

He turned and flew away.

At the foot of the volcano, eagle guards patrolled Zeta's lair. Leonard brought out an eagle costume called Harvey. Inside were levers and pedals that drove the suit.

While the rest of the heist crew walked safely into the base inside Harvey, Red and Silver sneaked in a different way ... and were caught!

Zeta sipped a tropical drink and glared cruelly at her prisoners. Red and Silver were trapped in the ice. Zeta's assistant, Debbie, turned on a huge TV screen, and the prisoners saw Piggy and Bird Islands. At the top of the screen was a countdown clock: **9:46.**

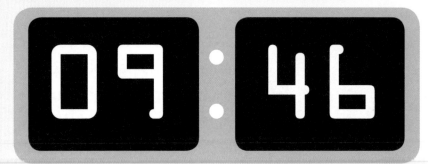

"When this countdown reaches zero, **BOOM!**" said Zeta. "Your islands are going down."

"Those islands are filled with innocent birds and pigs!" Red exclaimed.

"Not for long," Zeta replied.

But as soon as she and Debbie left ...

A huge explosion knocked down Zeta's door and released Red and Silver from the ice. It was Bomb and Chuck! Leonard, Garry and Courtney soon joined them.

Quickly, Red and Silver showed everyone the countdown.

"That's how long we've got till Zeta attacks both our islands," Silver explained. "We have to destroy the super weapon first."

The team planned to use one of the lava-filled ice balls, but then disaster struck. Debbie found that the prisoners had escaped.

"Glenn, begin the launch sequence!" Zeta commanded. "Bring me the launch button right now!"

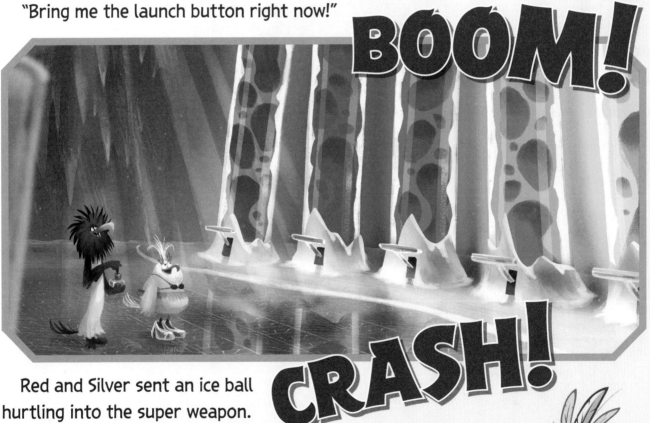

BOOM!

CRASH!

Red and Silver sent an ice ball hurtling into the super weapon.

The ice ball bounced off and smashed to pieces on the floor.

"It didn't work," Silver cried out.

"Of course it didn't work," Zeta said with a sneer. "Seize them!"

Silver and Red were prisoners again. Zeta lifted her talon, ready to stomp on the launcher. The islands were doomed!

To be continued ...

MAP MISSION

Leonard has sent Courtney to find the things he wants.
Help her by telling her which square each item is in.

A

BIRD ISLAND

B

C

D

BIRDLANTIC

E

PIGGY

OCEAN

N

F

W E

G

S

H
105° 90° 75° 60° 45° 30° 15°

1 2 3 4 5 6

38

1. Put your finger on each object and then run it along to the left side of the map.
2. Write down the letter that you find there.
3. Next, put your finger on the object and run it down to the bottom of the map.
4. Write down the number that you find there.

Now you have the map coordinates! The first one has been done for you below.

ISLAND

PIGCIFIC

OCE

Pink star	**C6**
Red crab	
Hot-air balloon	
Snake	
Egg shell	
Cup	
Slingshot	
Palm tree	

15°   30°   45°   60°   75°

7   **8**   **9**   **10**   **11**   **12**

SECRET CODE

Garry has invented a secret code so he can moan about Zeta without getting into trouble. (She just thinks he's doodling.)

Every letter of the alphabet has its own shape. By putting the shapes together, Garry can spell out anything he chooses.

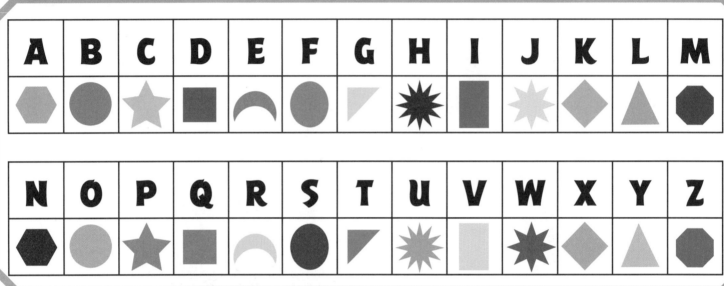

Garry has made a tower using Zeta's name. Create a tower of your own name. Then make some for your favourite Angry Birds.

Z
E
T
A

RUFFLE SOME FEATHERS

Join the dots to find out who Zeta is about to capture!

41

ANGRY BIRDS
Part Three

Everything stopped as Mighty Eagle swept down in front of Zeta.

"I'm the cause of all of this," he said. "I ran out on you on our wedding day. I ripped your heartstrings out."

"ZETA!" boomed a loud voice. **"WAIT!"**

That gave Red an idea.

"String!" he whispered to Silver. "Super String!"

Perhaps Silver's amazing invention could save the day?

Silver always had a piece of Super String with her. She gave it to Chuck, who zoomed up to the super weapon, put the string around the lava-filled ice ball in the launcher and then tied it to the floor.

Zeta was too busy yelling at Mighty Eagle to notice.

"You are nothing to me!" she screeched, her eyes filling with tears. Furious, she stomped on the launcher. The ice ball flew up towards the top of the volcano ... and then down again!

"RUN!"

The ice ball hit the super weapon with an almighty crash, and the volcano rumbled and shook. Birds and pigs ran. Eagles flew.

KABOOM!

The volcano had exploded. Eagle Island was in ruins, and everyone was covered in dust. For a moment, Zeta couldn't find her assistant Debbie anywhere. Then she saw that Mighty Eagle had shielded Debbie with his body. He had saved her life. Zeta's frozen heart began to thaw ...

Bird Island was more peaceful than ever before. Birds and pigs were living happily alongside each other.

So were Zeta and Mighty Eagle! He finally went through with their wedding, and a huge crowd of friends turned up to celebrate.

As for Red, he had led the team to victory, and he was a bigger hero than ever. He had everything he had ever wanted, but now he knew that it was lonely being a hero all by himself.

"Silver is the real hero," he told the birds of the island. "She saved all our lives."

"I didn't do this all on my own," Silver said.

"We're strongest when we band together," Red agreed, and nodded at Garry.

WHAT A TEAM!

THE END

45

EAGLE EYES

Zeta is training herself to recognise the birds and pigs if they creep up on her. Can you beat her time? Link each shadow with its owner in less than two minutes.

LEONARD

CHUCK

MIGHTY EAGLE

SILVER

RED

BOMB

5

2

6

1

3

4

46

Answers on page 52

KEEP IT COOL

Answers on page 52

CHILL OUT!

Debbie needs your help. She's lost on the iciest side of Eagle Island. Can you guide her home to the warm volcano?

START

SLINGSHOT SUPER QUIZ

How much do you remember about the birds' latest adventure? Answer these quick-fire questions at Chuck-speed and find out if you're a top swot or a brain drain. Good luck!

1. What hits a duck in the face at the beginning of the story?

2. What do the pigs drop onto the birds during the Prank War?

3. What colour is the balloon carrying Leonard's note?

4. Where does the heist crew meet for the first time?

5. What is Silver's amazing invention?

6. Zeta's lair is hidden inside what?

7. With what does Zeta fill her ice balls?

8. Who left Zeta on her wedding day, many years ago?

9. What is the name of Leonard's eagle disguise?

10. What time do Red and Silver see on the countdown clock?

11. Who rescues Red and Silver after they are captured?

12. What is the name of Zeta's top scientist?

13. What does Silver use to stop the ice ball from launching?

14. Whose life does Mighty Eagle save?

15. Who does Red say is the real hero?

14-15

It's official: you're a genius. Sign up for the Avian Academy immediately!

11-13

Not bad. You're almost as clever as Mighty Eagle thinks he is. Go and polish your trophies.

9-10

So you rushed your answers and missed out a few details. Who cares? It's just a great excuse to read the story again!

7-8

Don't lose your temper, but you're going to have to try a bit harder next time. BOOM!

4-6

Try reading the whole story, but not just the parts about the pigs. Remember, sometimes it takes two villages.

1-3

You're obviously too busy planning world domination to read the story. Better luck next time!

Answers on page 52

ANSWERS

PAGES 18-19
11 hatchlings are scampering around the pages.

PAGE 20
1. False.
2. True.
3. False.
4. True.
5. True.
6. False.
7. True.
8. True.
9. False.
10. False.

PAGE 27

Z	J	A	I	L	C	I	E	Q	H
A	W	H	R	A	Q	M	L	P	N
V	C	U	A	I	K	F	T	O	I
O	L	A	B	R	F	G	S	V	A
L	Q	S	D	J	B	I	A	J	T
C	H	C	A	E	B	O	C	X	N
A	F	I	K	Y	M	Z	U	S	U
N	M	T	L	I	H	Y	J	R	O
O	X	Y	J	U	N	G	L	E	M
V	I	L	L	A	G	E	D	F	K

PAGE 32
There are 23 pigs.

PAGE 33
1. RED
2. BOMB
3. SILVER
4. CHUCK
5. COURTNEY
6. ZETA
7. DEBBIE
8. MIGHTY EAGLE
9. GLENN
10. HATCHLINGS

PAGES 38-39

Pink star	**C6**
Red crab	**F3**
Hot-air balloon	**G9**
Snake	**B1**
Egg shell	**E10**
Cup	**D7**
Slingshot	**B7**
Palm tree	**B12**

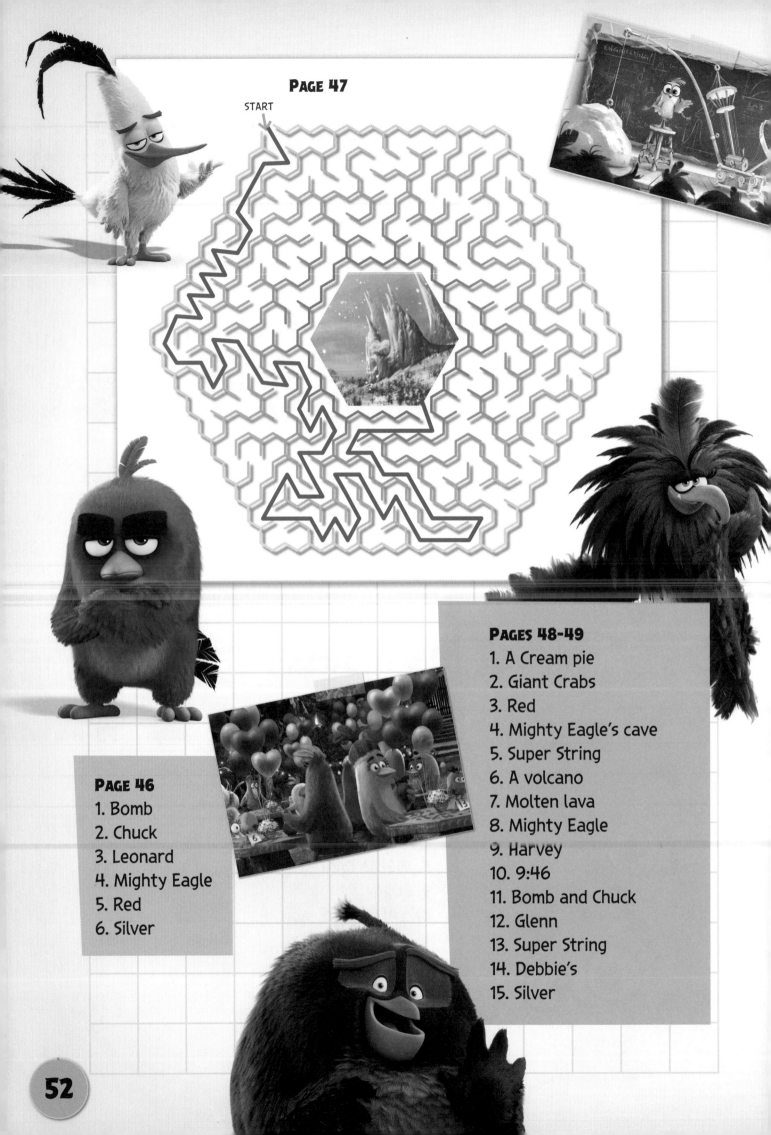

PAGE 47

START

PAGE 46
1. Bomb
2. Chuck
3. Leonard
4. Mighty Eagle
5. Red
6. Silver

PAGES 48-49
1. A Cream pie
2. Giant Crabs
3. Red
4. Mighty Eagle's cave
5. Super String
6. A volcano
7. Molten lava
8. Mighty Eagle
9. Harvey
10. 9:46
11. Bomb and Chuck
12. Glenn
13. Super String
14. Debbie's
15. Silver